Description (continued from back cover)

Alina and three fellow professionals, all young single women (two nurses, two teachers), are on vacation at a posh western US resort, enjoying sunshine, lake boating, and good cuisine. They chat and joke with nice fellow tourists, including handsome young men, on a street of lakefront bars with dancing, drinks, and dating opportunities.

Among those dancing in a crowded, throbbing sports bar is a silent young man you'd never notice unless you looked directly into his dark, crazed, hateful eyes. He is nameless, has a swastika tattoo, and never actually connects with other human beings or any other living creature for that matter. He is a sociopath, lacking conscience and social connectedness. Tonight, he chooses Alina as his target.

Mr. Swastika drops a pill into her drink, causing Alina to start hallucinating. Luckily, her friends get her safely back to the hotel before he can do any more harm or evil. But Alina's nightmare only begins as she falls into a feverish sleep filled with nightmare dreams in the Jurassic swamp that lies hidden in every person's subconscious jungle in the hinterlands of the brain. In this entertaining, thought-provoking story, Alina's nightmare reality takes on surprising dimensions and twists. While hunted by predators, she discovers her own inner tyrannosaur and becomes a force of roaring fury to be reckoned with.

description continues next page…

...description continues:

Sit in your backyard, or at the park, and watch for real: the killing zone of birds, butterflies, lizards, and small mammals. What we think is a lot of pleasant, peaceful chirping is really a chorus of battle signals. Every scent, every color, every wafting breeze holds its own life and death code...in very family's own Jurassic Backyard.

To save ourselves, we must open our eyes to understand the truth about our world, and about ourselves. Our heroine, Alina, is not only a talented and dedicated nurse but also an amateur history buff. In this story, she learns that the devil with the mustache and evil eyes (you know who; think swastika) and the young Jewish author of the children's classic Bambi did actually walk the same streets in pre-World War One Vienna. And Bambi holds dark secrets many of us never quite see past the cartoon colors...

(end of description; please begin reading...)

A Philosophical Dark Fantasy by John T. Cullen

Jurassic Backyard

Clocktower Books, San Diego California

Contact: editorial@clocktowerbooks.com.
Clocktower Books
P.O. Box 600973
Grantville Station
San Diego, CA 92160-0973.

CONTENTS

Preface 2020 (Vision Year)

I call this a Philosophical Novel, in the tradition of William Golding's The Inheritors or Lord of the Flies, to mention just two influences. The list of literary influences behind it is long. At the same time, it is an entertainment, a dark fantasy in the best traditions of popular fiction.

And, dear reader, I'm not given much to prefaces. I normally prefer to hop right into the story. So, let's get right into the story (Chapter 1: Garden) and save all the interesting, juicy background info for a detailed afterword following the amazing conclusion to this adventure fantasy about a professional nurse named Alina who travels to a wonderful, balmy, sunny resort with her friends on vacation – and encounters the dark side of reality -complete with Jurassic dinosaur teeth and an evil young man with Hitler tattoos, who clearly had not read Felix Salten's classic children's story Bambi, in which a cute little deer has a very dark encounter deep, deep in a forest...

Let's start reading, as Alina tells us her story.

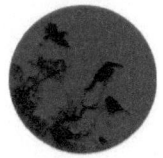

1. Garden

My name is Alina, and I was the victim of that evil young man with a swastika tattoo in the sports bar—of all places, in a wonderful seaside resort where my girlfriends and I were having such a nice evening. I'll never be the same again, but I'll survive.

I never heard the two tiny tablets being secretly dropped into my drink at a bar on the lake resort island. Nobody could later say they saw who did it, either. So nobody will ever go to jail for it, but not for the reason you might think.

I will forever carry inside me a vision of our world's reality and horror that I saw like a movie playing before me. No, with me in it, because I became one of the actors, the props, the scenery. It was terrifying. But this is what the truth really is, once you look beyond all the lies we tell ourselves to get through the day.

"Are you ready?" shouted three of my bright young women friends, while rapping loudly with their knuckles on my apartment door.

"Hold on," I shouted back while rushing around with a towel-turban on my head. I had a bath towel draped around my dripping torso, and nothing else over my birthday suit.

They stood laughing outside—bright, happy, looking forward to a fun evening on the town. They weren't going without me, which made me feel warm and included.

I slipped into my bathrobe and opened the door and said: "Hey!"

They all cheered. "Hey! Come on, Alina! Hurry up!"

They pushed past me into the apartment (actually, a time share that Dori and I were leasing for a week). The others were our friend Sheri and Laurel who joined us for Spring week.

Dori had gone upstairs to bring Sheri and Laurel down to ours from their time share apartment.

"Hold on, you guys," I said laughing. "Can't go in my bathrobe."

"Oh why not?" said outrageous Dori, who was already a little bit lit up with the local wine.

"I'd embarrass you," I said trying to sound logical while we were all being a little crazy already.

"The men are waiting," Sheri (the redhead) said.

"What men," her friend Laurel (brunette) scoffed. "Probably a bunch of losers." She didn't know how right she was.

"We need a blue eyed blonde along," said dark-haired Dori.

"Hold on," I said, "I have my dress all laid out on the bed. Help yourselves to some wine from the bar."

"Oh hey, yay," and so forth they all said. That got their attention, and I escaped to do my little bit of makeup and get dressed in the bed and bathroom suite.

Dori and I had managed to get this time share from a mutual friend, a nurse whose husband is a doctor back home at the city medical center. It was a big place, with two bedrooms that shared a full bath. The apartment also included a kitchen, dining room, and living room or den. The den had a large sliding glass door opening onto this fabulous patio, which in turn overlooked a quarter acre yard. That yard, which was carpeted with nicely mown grass, was studded with bushes (rosemary, brush cherry, and more) plus there were fruit trees (apple, plum, peach) buzzing with bees and birds of all types. Not to mention huge monarch butterflies flapping silently around in their ballet from blossom to blossom. The tall wooden privacy fence all around was offset with attractive pear trees and bushes.

When the girls arrived, it was just on the verge of dusk. You could see past the yard, overlooking the broad expanse of that beautiful lake dotted with little sails of all fun colors. The sun just then made a huge floating peach sort of splash on a perfect blue sky on the horizon. It was gorgeous. So peaceful, tranquil, harmonious, you name it.

As I quickly dressed in my dark, flowered, short summer dress, I could hear the other three in the living room. Sheri said: "If I were an artist, I'd sit out there on the patio with watercolors and capture the scene."

"That sunset in the garden is so glorious," Laurel said.

"Not to mention how the lake sparkles like liquid gold and peach melba," Dori added.

There was a show on about Vienna, the capital of Austria, back in time just before World War One, so we're talking about 1907 to 1913. I'd seen it before, and found that overall epoch in history fascinating. But I'm not just a working nurse (N.P., M.S.) but also famous among my friends as a history nerd, and I love that stuff. It's not just about wars and marching bands, not just about strutting emperors and millions of dead soldiers and destroyed lives—all for nothing, as usual, so typically dinosaurs and Jurassic and Cretaceous and all that. I could imagine them all roaring in their swamps, hungry for blood.

It's about fashion, dancing, *Moulin Rouge* (Red Windmill in the Montmartre of Paris, as in Can-Can, oo-la-lah!) and all that new Ragtime jazzy stuff coming over from the U.S.A.

Those decades were the *Belle Époque*, French for

Beautiful Era. It wasn't so beautiful if you were a maid working below stairs, or a young man shoveling coal in a mine, but it was a time of great creativity and huge money (the peak of the European and North American world empire) and a lavish celebration before it all came crashing down in a dark hail of artillery and machine guns, of poison gas and bombs dropped from those new-fangled *aeroplanes* of canvas and wood, and heavy steel tanks clanking through the mud... Before the world wars, it was an age when fashion designers like Coco Chanel could rise from nothing and make beautiful dresses and immortal perfumes in Paris. It was a time of great composers, painters, singers, dancers were celebrating up a storm in great cities like Paris, London, New York, and Vienna and more. Huge story, I love the whole TV series.

I'd seen that one particular episode of the series before. It talks about how two souls breathed the same air in Vienna for about seven years. One was Felix Salten, who wrote a powerful story called *Bambi, A Life in the Woods*, published in 1923 in Vienna, which was made into a sanitized 1942 Walt Disney classic animated film.

The other, a truly dark spirit who arrived in Vienna as a young man of 18 and left seven years later in 1913 (just before World War One started in 1914) was Adolf Hitler. He was a disturbed, hateful, angry spirit who knocked on doors around Vienna, wanting to become a great painter. He was refused entry, because he lacked the education and talent (more specifically, any sort of real human soul). So he became a starving vagrant, picking up day labor where he could. In his spare time, he painted rather pedestrian little watercolor souvenirs that (how ironic) he sold for a few *Groschen* (coins) to mostly Jewish shopkeepers who took pity on him. But oh how he would get even on all of them and nearly destroy the world in doing so.

Felix Salten (born Siegmund Salzmann, son of an Orthodox Jewish rabbi) had moved to Vienna with his family shortly after his birth in 1869 in Pest, which is half of the fabulous city of Buda-Pest in Austria-Hungary. The family soon moved to Vienna (capital of the Austro-

Hungarian empire) because Jews received full citizenship and toleration in Vienna. That was during the *Belle Époque*, that wonderful period in so many ways, at least for the rich and the creative across Europe in the decades before the blood bath began (two world wars, over a hundred million dead for no reason except the testosterone madness of Kaiser Bill in Germany and later Adolf Hitler, a rewind of same stuff but on even greater steroids). Argue all you want about exact causes, this and that, but the dead don't live to enjoy any more sunshine, and most of them were innocent young lives snuffed out for always the wrong reasons.

Adolf Hitler certainly lit a fire that torched much of the world, already scorched from earlier wars in that Unbeautiful Era from 1914 to 1945.

Felix Salten was in his thirties by the time he started writing and selling stories after 1900. He was approaching forty when that anonymous evil spirit floated into the imperial capital amid all of its Waltz music and glory. In those days, the armies were resting, and the generals were gearing up for their next glories. Uniforms were splendid, sparkling with gold medals earned on parade grounds rather than muddy battlefields. What wars they fought were in distant realms of their empires, in remote corners of Africa or Asia. It was a time for fairy tales, and Felix Salten dialed into all that.

In the Germanic world, if you think of the Brothers Grimm, fairy tales were indeed grim. And if you think of how German the English really were (all their royals, from the Georges to Prince Albert to Queen Victoria) had family names like Hannover and Saxe-Coburg, which the English royals had to quickly change to Winsor or risk getting booted out by the English. Never mind that England is Angle-land, named for the Germanic invaders who took over after the Romans left in the 400s. But then again, France is named for a German nation (the Franks) so history is filled with bloody ironies.

So there I am, powdering my nose and humming lightly to myself, with all that bloody history playing out in my memory. It's important, like I said, because the date rape drug I was given by Mr. Swastika, that son of a bitch, made me hallucinate in 360 degree Technicolor, and it was horrible. I'll get to all that shortly. And I'll talk about Felix Salten's great creation, Bambi, the most famous little deer in history.

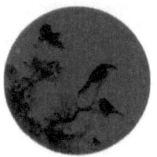

I checked myself out in the bedroom with the door partially open, twirling before the tall mirror on the bathroom door.

Dori and I each had a single bed, and between us was a generous French door leading out to that wonderful slate-flagstone patio with wrought iron table and wiry chairs. The table outside had a glass top, and standing in the middle was a red and white striped umbrella. The chairs, like the table, were wound-steel painted elegant black, glossy, and quite ritzy like everything else in the condo complex and for that matter the town below by the lake.

Minutes later, having sat before the bathroom mirror with some light applicators (a little mauve dust around the eyes, blink-blue, a touch of mascara in the lashes, and a quick dusting of peachy dust on the cheekbones, a little help from a quick reddish lift upward on the cheeks), and I rose, ready to do battle.

The girls all whistled and clapped admiringly as I stepped back into the den, where they sat on plush furniture with the local TV news on while they sipped wine. That was the dark red, blood-colored wine from my nurse friend's cabinet, in expensive glowing crystal stemmed glasses.

I plopped down to buckle on my white strap-up quarter-heel shoes. I sometimes wear taller heels, but when you have a bit of wine, and want to go dancing (assuming a suitable man approaches you), I don't want to be wobbling around on stilettos. The other girls were all dressed similarly—summery, sensible, with dressy practical shoes.

"What's on the news?" I said casually, not really caring. It was just conversation.

"Same old," said Sheri, the palest-skinned of us, with freckles like spattered orange juice. I'm the blonde, but I have more Latina skin than Sheri, who looks more Germanic or English or Irish. We're all mixes, right? Dori is part Asian, with dark almond-shaped eyes and glossy black hair. Laurel is a brunette of Italian extraction and a bit of Afro in the mix.

"Same old violence, murder, shootings, rapes..." Dori added.

"Oh stop," Laurel said, cutting her off. "I don't want t hear it."

"We want to have fun," Sheri said.

"Like that old song," Laurel said. "Girls just want to have fun."

We all sang a brief refrain, girls... *just a-want to have fun, oh, oh...*

We all laughed. We were having fun. So far. It was all looking good.

While I was getting ready in the bedroom, they watched TV in the living room. I caught glimpses of the big TV from my bedroom vanity as I fussed about to look pretty.

The television was on, and this is important as I later realized, while recovering from the soon to be madness in a resort bar overlooking the lake, where a young man with a swastika tattoo and icy Arctic eyes slipped some of his hate and cruelty into my fizzy little pink drink. I'll explain part now, part later...

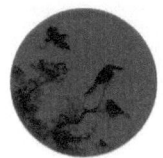

Soon after, the four of us marched down the main steps onto the broad, clean sidewalks and streets of this fragrant, summery resort.

It was nighttime by now. The last faint glow of dusk shone dimly on the horizon, while the lake waters had become an unfathomable blackness livened up by a few gently churning, brightly lit tour boats out for the evening dinner and dancing cruise.

The four of us were renting two condos in this building just for the week. There were about two hundred other time shares and apartments in this huge, sprawling white complex with its brick-red roofs nestled amid thick tree crowns.

It's a town where rich people from all over the world come to sit in the sun, sail on the lake, gamble a little at the casino nearby, go for drives in the hills and woods, or just enjoy the rustling of palm trees, the smell of night-blooming jasmine, the splashing of blue water sparkling with sunlight.

Locals here can make pretty good money as waiters, waitresses, drivers, and all the usual resort occupations. It's pretty much the same as that *Belle Époque* stuff, come to think of it. How different do things really ever get? The rich come to party, do drugs, do deals, have their way. The poor work below stairs and run around saying *yessir, yes ma'am*, while hoping for a good tip. Then they spit in the bushes and move on to the next song and dance for a few coins. I worked with a concierge office in a big hotel back home while I was busting my cheeks going to nursing school not long ago. I learned much at first hand about valets, doormen, housekeeping, and all the rest of the honest work ordinary folks do to stay alive, and still manage to have fun and smile brightly as wealthy folks tip us (or don't; whatever).

But don't get me wrong. I keep it light and have fun. It's just that the background noise (history, Adolf, Bambi) was making faint music in my subconscious the whole time as I stepped out with my girlfriends. It was all about to come back, haunting me...

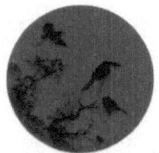

We were having a nice time that evening. As the hour grew late, we managed to stay reasonably sober, just having a pleasant buzz. A few men (some too old, some too young, nobody just right) asked us to dance, and we did as isolated singles. It was a laid back, easy going evening until about eleven.

Who knows what happens around that time. Maybe the boaters come back from the lake, and the drivers return from the countryside. A lot of locals get off work, and everyone is out to have a last glass or two, a couple of wild dances while the DJs spin their albums or whatever, and the waiting staff get a lot of exercise rushing through the crowd holding their trays high.

At some point, we four girls stood together debating if we should retire for the night, get a good sleep, and work on that tan by the cabanas at the lake tomorrow. We really didn't want to call it a night yet, so we agreed to each have just one more glass of wine. From this particular lakeside resort and casino, it was a walk of about three blocks back to the complex where Dori and I shared an apartment, and Laurel and Sheri had a similar pad on the deck above.

We stood within view of the lake, where at this hour I could see tour boats draped in multi-colored lights slowly and gracefully cruising up and down. The loudspeakers in our venue were loud, but not deafening. You could hear bits of music pounding and wafting over the waters from the lake.

The multiple French doors all stood open, letting in a cool, fragrant night air.

And of course we were aware of the eyes upon us. Some of the men were locals, while others were from money and out of town. At this hour, all blended together, it was hard to tell them apart. The money mingled with the townie, and they all sought the honey (that was us).

We commented among each other that some of the guys were tall and attractive, a few almost like movie stars, but as Dori said, too many hard eyes, too much hunting in those looks. All four of us are professionals. I'm a nurse practitioner or NP, Dori is an RN, while Sheri and Laurel are both high school teachers with M.A. degrees. It's not that we're stuck up, but we are definitely choosy. We're single, in our early twenties, and certainly open to meeting someone nice. I don't think any of us were seeing that sort of guy, not even Dori who was a drink or two ahead of the rest of us.

That's when everything changed for me.

2. Adolf and Bambi

You don't notice it coming on at first. It's late. You're tired. You think: *wow, am I feeling extra tired all of a sudden?*

I had this feeling almost as if I'd walked into the lake and was underwater.

I heard voices talking and couldn't see people around me anymore.

I knew by then that something was very wrong.

"She's wasted," Shari said.

"Let's get her home," Laurel said.

"You go girl," Dori said. "Oh come on, honey… Alina… what's wrong, baby? I drank more than you did, and you can always hold your own."

A disembodied womanly voice I didn't recognize said from somewhere in the black, swirling lake water all around me: "There have been some guys putting things in women's drinks lately."

Another woman's voice floated behind that one: "Date rape drugs. Better get her home to bed."

That's the last intelligible thing I heard until I was back at the apartment lying flat on my back.

"That stuff stays in your system half a day or more. She may still be flashing off and on again tomorrow."

I know somehow I barfed into a bucket held by one of my friends.

I thought I was going to drop my face into that bucket with it, but they toweled my features clean and let me pass out on my bed. At least I was safe and sound, with protective friends, so I let go and hoped I'd be back to normal in the morning.

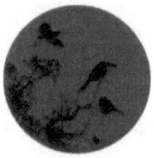

When you have dreams on a trip like that, you don't remember much about them later.

All I know is that I was terrified, and running the whole time.

Picture an old sepia film, full of floating rips and tears in morgue-white.

I had fleeting but persistent mental snapshots of Adolf Hitler, mustache and all, with those black merciless eyes behind which there was no normal human soul. And that lipless, cruel mouth that stupid people think represents power and justice, but is carved from a wooden mask of Satan. Just a sociopath, a sick and narcissistic toddler who never grew up, who plays into the worst instincts of village idiots and drives them to murder and violence as his whims dictate, and the rich clap loudly and laugh as they make billions in the war industries.

As I reflect on all this long afterward, when I'm recovered from the nightmare and moving on with my life, I know this also. There is a Hitler number (about 37%) that represents how many votes the Nazis actually go in the 1933 elections. Hitler wasn't elected. He was appointed at the demand of the bankers, the industrialists, and the militarists because they thought they could manage him (even though they loathed him and looked down on him, as they had done with Kaiser Bill a generation earlier). The zillionaires, the ambitious and ruthless, live in the moment like any sociopath. They want money and power, and they want it now. They don't care about consequences, whether next moment or a few years out when all of society lies in rubble and ruins with a corpse odor that gags and nauseates you from miles away.

Also in that mental nightmare (thanks to Mr. Adolf in

that bar) I had flashbacks to Bambi, and it wasn't a warm fuzzy cartoon with Flower and Thumper the Bunny and Friendly Owl, and the other little forest creatures. It was a rather typical dark Germanic nightmare full of foreboding, like the Grimm stories or, from across the Channel, English nightmares like Alice in Wonderland or those English nursery rhymes. Since ancient times, grandmothers have told mythic stories to children, to arouse their sense of wonder, to put them to dreamy sleep, and above all to teach them moral lessons by scaring them silly. Until modern times, people weren't really children; they were little people who had to work from the earliest age, most of them got no education, and there really wasn't any such thing as childhood, at least officially if you listened to how the world was run by predatory dukes and pukes, who rode around on horses, wore medals, and owned factories and sailing vessels in addition to all the land. As the children of more recent ages grew up, and got to take charge of their story telling, they demanded warm and fuzzy stories to warm the heart, so all those old nightmare tales got sanitized. But those dark realities live in the gloomy swamps of our subconscious, where they were born, and come out to haunt us when we are hallucinating (like on a serious date rape drug, as I was).

What saved me, I am sure, is my fundamental belief that we are capable of both the worst and the best, and as long as we strive for the best, we can live lives of virtue and kindness and sunshine. I clung to that faith the whole time.

So Bambi is this little deer in the 1923 story, whose mommy got knocked up by one of the Great Princes among deer (who have their fun and then saunter off to do antler stuff among each other, while the females are left to raise the young). Bambi doesn't meet his dad until later in the story.

There was enough of the original in the cleaned-up, animated Disney film to make me weep as a little girl when I first saw it. That came from a time (1942) at the darkest points in World War Two, when Hitler had not yet been defeated. The world still teetered in desperation and uncertainty. The great victory had not yet risen out of darkness. The world still bore that same darkness that spawned Adolf's bloody vision in early 1900s Vienna and then Munich, where he joined the Royal Bavarian army and fought for the Kaiser in Berlin.

In those years, Adolf and Bambi breathed the same air of a soon to vanish imperial fantasy that would be replaced by far darker nightmares before the coming of gray dawn in 1945.

The real moral of Bambi is one that has been picked up by conservationists and earth-savers (hurray, I am one of them). Namely, the bad guys are humans. Add to that: we're only bad guys as long as we follow the dark side of our souls, led by stern-faced crazy guys of whom there are plenty to go around in every age (like Kaiser Bill, or Adolf, or that same type of smelly monster eating the world alive today with the help of his village idiot supporters who are there in every age of history, ready to lynch and to riot and to burn cities and to kill as many 'hated others' as they can, once old Stern-Face has put the empty but burning terror in their blind little minds, always with the help of religion gone bad).

Bambi's sweet momma raises her little fawn in the safety of the deep, dark woods. Then, as he begins to feel his oats (or his nuts?), she takes him (cautiously) into the open, sunny meadows with all of their dangers (yet lots of cute female deers or dears to scamper with).

The great terror of Felix Salten's story is a horrifying, shadowy creature the animals call simply He, also known as The Man, who comes with a gun and kills innocent forest creatures. Like any carnivore, he then takes it home to his den, and devours his kill along with his mate and offspring.

You guessed it. The Man shoots at Bambi, but misses. He kills Bambi's momma. So poor little Bambi lies sobbing and crying with his head on his dying momma's belly as she coughs and breathes her last breaths. Nothing warm and fuzzy about that dark cartoon. I cried when I first saw the movie in a European theater years ago.

She whispers her last words to her little guy: "I love you, Bambi. Mommy loves you. Be good and stay safe. Find a nice little girl deer, and look for your daddy. He's the Great

Prince of Deers and he'll take care of you." And then she dies, leaving Bambi (and kids like me watching) forever with a broken heart.

Felix Salten continued with a very gloomy, sober story in which Bambi has a rather sad marriage with a lovely deer named Farina, among other almost-romances and bar-hopping around the forest and meadows. He has to do the antler thing to destroy other stags who are bullying him (so human, while not humane). He becomes the Prince of Deer himself, when he is old enough. In the end, he's got the putz and the nuts and nobody can give him any buts. But he's not a happy prince nor a happy stag, and...

...yeah, *whatever*...

I just wonder if The Man, as he raises his gun and fires, is wearing a Hitler mustache. Wouldn't surprise me.

Is there anything we can do to save this world from the insanity in our swamp?

What if The Woman came along, about six feet tall and wearing armor and waving a sword. What if *She* kicked The Man's ass from one end of the meadow to the other, and broke his gun over his *Klotz* of a head while he cowered there, whining pitifully and holding his tattoo-covered skull like the coward that he really is?

Well, listen to the rest of my story. I can't explain it, but for a short time I became The Woman...

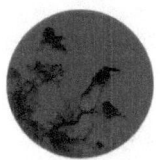

Lo and behold, about noon, I woke up.

I couldn't remember much of anything. The dream stuff would only come back to me later in flashbacks, and even those would fade in a few weeks. I just remember enough now, months later, to laugh about it (in a sad way sort of, but glad the sunshine is back, and the Jurassic is gone from the

Yard).

As I woke up, the aching and dizziness and nausea were mostly gone. I had slept well.

I could hear birds twittering the sunshine outside on the patio, and a sweet smell of flowers came in on a balmy breeze.

It felt soooo good to be alive.

"Hey, sleepy head," Dori said. She sat by the bed, sipping coffee and munching on a roll.

Laurel stepped in from the patio. "Is she awake?"

"How are you feeling?" Sheri asked from the closet area in the bedroom, where she was trying out a light blue silk slip.

"Not too bad, actually."

Something told me I wasn't quite done with that dark movie in my head, but this was progress.

Afraid I was going to be sick again, I slowly sat up. They had taken my dirtied, barfy dress off, and put some jogging shorts and a T-shirt on me before letting me pass out into a deep sleep.

I was in good hands. I'm sure Dori (experienced E.R. nurse) was watchful, in case I needed ambulance transportation, which apparently I did not.

"Need to barf some more?" Laurel asked. "I cleaned out the bucket last night."

Sheri rushed over holding the freshly empty bucket. "Here it is."

"Thanks, guys." I smacked my lips and moved my head slowly from side to side like a radio antenna, listening to secret airwaves. "Nope. If anything, I'm a little hungry."

"Girl, you emptied out everything you ever ate," Dori said. "We had to change your clothes for you too. Here, try some dry bread. If that works, we can add a little marmalade. No butter for you."

The thought of anything greasy made me cringe. I took the slice of crusty bread she offered, and nibbled on it gratefully. It tasted fresh and bready and so good. "Mmmmhh."

"Wonderful," Dori said in a motherly and R.N. fashion.

"I'll make you another one with strawberry compote."

"Sounds great," I said.

"Some tea," Sheri suggested. "No coffee. Nothing acidic."

"Sparkling water to make her belch," Laurel said. "That's what you need. Soda and bitters. Old bartender remedy for upset stomach."

I laughed. "All of the above, girls."

I moved into the living room and wrapped myself in a blanket, sitting on the couch.

"She is feeling better," Shari said gratefully.

"We were so worried," Laurel said. "I was on the phone with hotel security, and they said they are looking at security cam footage but it's dark and grainy. They apologized, and said they are aware that some bastards are doing this to people, to women, and they're going to keep a sharper eye on things."

"Oh thanks a lot too late," Dori said in her usual acid tone.

"Bunch of effing predators!" Shari said.

Dori added: "Had a call from the emergency department at the local hospital. They were asked to call us by the hotel management. The doctor I spoke with said to bring you in if you get bad again."

"I'm feeling much better," I said.

"The doctor said if it's the new date rape drug they've seen, it's a powerful hallucinogen. You could have some flashes or scary visions for another day or so. It comes and goes."

"Wonderful," I said with a tone more bitter than I cared to feel. "Whoever did this to me, *up yours*."

Sheri shook her head. "What ever possesses a guy… or a chick, I guess? What do they get out of it?"

"Certainly not a date," Laurel said with comical finality.

We all laughed rather bitterly, but with a sense of triumph to have survived on the Meadow.

It felt good to laugh and be surrounded by such good friends.

One of the girls brought me a hot, steaming cup of tea, and that did wonders for my stomach.

The ladies fussed around, and pretty soon there was Laurel trying on a wide-brimmed straw hat.

"Perfect for the beach," Sheri said.

"We should go for a walk. That sunlight is so toasty and the breezes are so balmy."

"I can hear palm trees rustling," Dori said. She looked my way. "Are you feeling up for a walk?"

I shook my head. "No longer nauseous or dizzy, but I don't have a lot of energy. You girls go ahead."

"Would you mind?" Laurel said almost pleadingly.

Sheri sat beside me and pressed her cell phone in my palm. "We're going to go for a walk. We'll be gone an hour, no more than two. If you need anything, just call us, okay?"

I clutched the phone thankfully. "I will. You guys go have a blast."

So, within about ten minutes, with a lot of loud chatter and laughing, they happily departed.

After the door slammed, and their sandals stopped echoing on the floor in the corridor outside, I rose and went to the kitchen. I felt a bit like older, or middle-aged, or something. Keeping the blanket wrapped around myself, I heated water and poured myself a second cup of that wonderful amber tea.

I cautiously nibbled at some ph-neutral and ph-positive foods (no acids), and got some protein down including a little cottage cheese, yoghurt, and slivered almonds. I sipped tea, and nibbled on salty crackers. That made me feel better.

Shuffling at a leisurely pace, I walked through the French doors, outside onto the beautiful patio with its bluish, grayish slate stones, with a few tea-colored ones inset as well. I didn't go to the table and umbrella set, but to one of several green and white striped beach chairs on wooden frameworks.

I still felt a bit woozy at random moments, but just briefly.

Once or twice, I thought I might blow lunch again, but it was a faint, passing sense. I recalled what Dori said the doctor said about flashbacks. I knew that some small percentage of our species are sociopaths with no human feelings or bonding, who would get a rise out of causing hurt in someone just for the hell of it. That includes a certain type of jealous spider (woman), or those nasty guys who can't get a date with a decent woman, so they (snakes) resort to stealthy cruelty and laugh at the victim's suffering. It's all part of the antler thing. We are idiots, but we can rise above it, with the right leadership, if the village idiots don't kill them off in favor of the stern-faced mass murderers and fake scripture thumpers they so prefer in their insect minds.

What ever, I thought, get over it and move on.

It was so reassuring to have my friends, and to know they rescued me. The guy who did this, if it was a guy (rather than a jealous woman who hated blondes or something), was probably the type who couldn't get a date and got his under-sized antlers *shtupped* on the Meadow.

Served him right. Or her. I didn't think I'd ever know, or care.

Yeah, but…

I cradled my tea cup in both hands, enjoying its warmth. I loosened the blanket, because the sunlight was really getting quite warm. I actually rose and walked over to sit at the table, in the shade of that gaily striped umbrella.

Out on the lake, many little sails blossomed in triangular shapes, each a white or green or red testimony to what a good time the vacationing men and women on board must be having.

In the middle of the lake was a larger motorboat, anchored and with scuba diving buoys around it. It was too far to see men and women jumping off with their tanks and fins.

Traffic drove past on the shore road, about two or three blocks below the hill on which this property sat. Behind me, the condos loomed with benign stateliness.

Except for the gently blowing wind, and an occasional distantly droning propeller plane or sightseeing helicopter, the atmosphere was very still.

I began to feel almost as if I were the only person in the world.

While I enjoyed the stillness and solitude around me, I could enjoy the smaller things.

Hummingbirds came and went, stopping here and there with blurry wings to inspect a red blossom.

Big monarch butterflies (and other models) fluttered about from flower to flower.

There were indeed lots of blossoms open to the bright daylight, offering themselves to the birds and insects to nourish themselves on the nectar while at the same time spreading the seeds about to help the flowers reproduce.

Big fat bees droned about.

Sparrows zipped about, looking for places to eat and to

nest.

I took a deep breath, sighed, and enjoyed being part of this world, a functioning member of this entire happy living club.

I might have just begun to doze, because I started slipping into a fragmented dream in which ants and termites browsed in their underground cities. Worms slithered about in the earth like subway trains. A snake silently undulated under the flowers, looking maybe for a mouse to eat. A rat nuzzled in a woodpile.

And right about there is when the strangeness set in.

The world got really weird.

3. Jurasssic Yard

It was noon, so why the dusky twilight all around me?

I opened my eyes and shrieked.

The light remained dazed and dimmed and tea-colored.

I dropped my teacup, which spilled and shattered on the slate patio.

On a wall nearby sat a large grayish-white bird, a falcon maybe, eyeballing me with raptor eyes. He was looking at me as if gauging how best to attack me.

But why?

I knew pretty quickly that reality had set in, maybe with the help of that drug somehow. Or was that low, foul stench really a muzzy, humid air tainted with blood and humus?

This was the real world—a Jurassic Yard.

Overhead, a flight of blackbirds attacked a stately pair of broad-winged hawks sailing by on tan wings.

An armored lizard flicked out its tongue and killed a darting moth.

Spiders wove silently pulsating nets in whose sticky symmetry a bee was stuck and wriggling in its death dance.

There was no peace here, just an endless killing field.

Every living thing was in a constant, terrorized battle for survival and procreation.

Even the flowers competed with each other, so those getting more nutrients under the ground could overwhelm the weaker ones and steal their sunlight, leaving them to wither and die in the shadow (below stairs) of their flowering glory and success.

The birds had a strategy. Their nest, with helpless young, was hidden under a roof beam under the building's balcony behind me. The male of the nesting pair (mourning doves) stayed with the nest to protect it from predatory bird species. The dove's mate was out looking for food. When the female returned, she did not fly to the nest. Instead, she landed on a tree and looked carefully about to see if she had been followed. When she saw that the coast was clear, she quickly flew in the straight line to the nest. They don't read books or think about it. They have instinct, which is a hard-wired instruction set based on eons of hard experience.

A hawk landed on a tree limb elsewhere in the yard. It spread its wings to hide its catch from other birds overhead, including its own kind. It would look left, then right, and quickly dip its head take a beakful bite of the dead sparrow clutched in one set of claws, while clutching the branch with its other claws. Everything about it, from the sharply hooked beak to the razor talons, was a weapon.

And the way evolution had slowly run through the numbers and things had sorted themselves out, birds and other flying creatures were almost safe from the prowling ground traffic: cute, furry cats with saber teeth and ripping claws. Who had to run from dogs with power-jaws and teeth capable of breaking bones if they caught a cat or other small mammal.

The insects underground in their teeming hives were protected (up to a point) until gophers dug their way through and made a feast of thousands. Same with ants, and those pretty black May flies with red dots all over their wing shells.

The light grew dimmer and darker, maybe because I was looking through new eyes. My vision was that of some evolutionary ancestor eons ago, whose primary weapons were smell and taste rather than vision and interpretation. The smell of an approaching killer was more immediate than triangulating the flight of a raptor bird. But the choice of weapons varies from species to species.

Which is why the hunting hawk hovers slowly, and has eyes sharp enough to spot a mouse far below. The bird has one eyed vision (not binocular with two eyes) and plunges down fast as gravity will take it, barely rustling its frozen and tattered-looking wing feathers, to nail that little rodent with a beak the way a spear fishing human will shoot a turtle or a wriggling eel.

I rose, making a silent scream with my wide open mouth.

I held my palms to my tortured temples and felt instinct take over from reason.

My movement scared off the big grayish-white bird, who abruptly sailed away without any wasted motion, looking for an easier if less meaty kill.

I was safe for the moment. But for how long?

As I stood on the patio, I was flooded by thoughts and by emotions (instincts) from all sides.

I was an apex predator. We had killed or driven off or put in zoos all our potential rivals. We were (largely) safe in our towns and cities from animals that had terrified our ancestors until very recently (and still did in more remote parts of the world).

We forgot about those little micro thingies that inhabit our guts. I'm a nurse and I see it every day. We keep the micro bugs under control, and some of them living in our blood, in our tunnels, are friendly (for the moment) helping us fight off flu, Ebola, leprosy, whatever...

I was less inclined to worry about a tiger or a crocodile or a bear *than*...

...*oh yes, another human.* Truly our worst fear, the most frightful plague of all.

Like the predator who put those pills in my drink last night.

As a woman, I must live in fear every day of my life from every man I encounter, wondering at first moment if he was about to rape me, or use his superior strength and speed to steal my purse; or maybe just kill me (being a coward, only if nobody is looking) for the fun of seeing another living thing suffer and drain of its life force, like small boys blowing up frogs with straws up the rear end and other horrors.

In most cases, the men I encounter turn out to be either protectors or indifferent, and each moment of dread passes quickly.

The smart male knows his best chance of survival and procreation is to treat the female well, and to nurture his offspring. They are the majority. It's that tiny minority of snakes and spiders who create all the destruction and terror; whenever they gain the upper hand, it's Berlin 1945 all over again (rubble sinking of corpses, from horizon to horizon).

I don't go anywhere alone. As much as possible, I keep company with other women to avoid being alone with a man I don't know or whose motives aren't clear enough...

...until or unless (and it happens occasionally) I am in the clutches of a female sociopath who works differently but just as terrifyingly. She may attack, but more often she will be the manipulator on a school playground, agitating the dumbest of the children through fear and hate until they run in a herd and become violent predators; village idiots in the making, same pattern. Playground violence will start as taunting, until one or two real savage bullies (boys often older, bigger, held back a year or two) cannot overcome their raptor instincts and resort to naked, sweaty, glistening muscular kicking, beating, and punching, while the kid who is 'different' lies on his back and his broken glasses are nearby, or maybe it's his crutches, or whatever makes him different. In later life, these same manipulators become the demagogues who lead idiots and fools in false crusades that overthrow governments and lead armies in senseless, brainless wars against neighboring tribes or nations, only to typically end in oceans of rubble as far as the eye can see in less than a decade. Idiots, who have no knowledge and no critical thinking skills, cannot form an opinion. Rather, what they mistake for their 'opinion' is really an Emotion, formed for them by their manipulators. Most often, false (dark, violent, hateful) perversions of religion are the most powerful and useful tool to turn these simpletons into useful fools to make oligarchs and tyrants wealthier. The sad thing is that, with good leadership (not Hitler or Mussolini types) the result can be years of relative peace like in the optimistically named Wonderful Era (if you don't look too closely at the many industrial-imperial horrors all around the world).

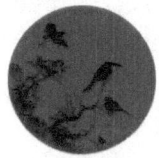

As a Nurse Practitioner, I have seen in my young years what humans do to each other. We see it every day in the Emergency Rooms: shot, stabbed, broken, beaten, burned, run over... adults and children alike. Not counting the more subtle things humans do to each other, all the emotional and mental abuse that leaves no visible scars except if you know what to look for in behavioral abnormalities (which leave the victims, especially children, further open to brainless abuse on the playground).

As an educated woman, I also studied history and read literature and knew that every generation must learn the same tragic lesson again on its own. It's called the Human Condition.

One of my favorites is in a dusty book published long ago by a folksy philosopher named Ann Landers, who wrote: *We are Stone Age people living in an Atomic Age society.*

Nothing ever changes. And here we are again, as always, starting over from the bare essentials.

And here I was, with darkness flooding my eyes and a droning filling my ears, as from a thousand bees, thanks to that unknown monster or monsters last night at that bar.

Or was he (they) as unknowable as I wanted to think?

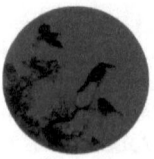

As I held my head pressed between white, desperate palms and uttered a silent scream, I caught fragmented flashbacks of those cold, insect-like lizard eyes of the men looking at us.

It was starting to come back to me, because I really wanted to know who did this to me.

I saw them or him, whatever... I just blocked it out, avoiding it, as a woman will do, as a human being will do with things too unpleasant to consciously dwell upon with the reasoning mind.

I saw him (them)...

...staring in cold hunger at me, the way that bird had just eyeballed me to see if I'd make a quick snack.

Predators.

My hyperactive brain sorted through thousands of snapshots of men's faces, of dark eyes in white eyeballs, of all manner of faces from narrower to rounder ones, with longer noses or shorter ones, with brown or black or kinky or slicked back hair. With mustache or beard or just bluish shadow needing a shave. In those fleeting seconds and that cutting room floor sequence, I did spot one face...

...I must have noticed him and looked away in utter loathing.

He had a smirk. That alone is nauseating, and cuts like a knife.

Oh, and his eyes were like cold chisel points, carving away at my soul. He had no soul, just a hunger to hurt and dominate and maybe kill.

He was a sociopathic predator, a human-like creature with no soul. He was more of an insect, a spider throbbing patiently in its web, waiting for a passing victim to get stuck and die a slow, agonizing death. Or maybe one of those female spiders that eats the male while they are having sex (he gets one final orgasm for his trouble, before she tears his head off and his world goes forever dark; and she gets a lot of protein to strengthen up her eggs). That face... something about him... He was with three companions, all woman-haters, with those dirty grins that the wolf pack or bully mob shows as they destroy the weak one in their pack.

The guy staring at me had a short, dirty-blond, almost military looking haircut. He had a tattoo of a swastika on his closely shaven temple on the right side. I could figure out that he would let his hair grow over it most of the time, until he was ready to go hunting, with this three beta males following closely. He'd show his colors by shaving the hair along the sides of his head. Maybe it was a prison thing. Sure, he seemed like the kind of male who spent years in prison, learning the whole spider and snake culture there to replace any sort of civilized (or what passes for civil) social norms on the Outside.

I got a fleeting glimpse of his three accomplices as well. They all had short haircuts and some form of tattoo, although theirs were gang symbols on the neck. Mr. Swastika was the leader...

Now I had a clearer memory of who did this to me.

No evidence that would hold up in court.

And I had long ago decided I was not the type of person to get a gun and go hunting for revenge. As abhorrent as that idea was to me to begin with, filling a person with the acid sickness of hate and anger, nothing could outweigh the terrifying idea that I might shoot the wrong person, an innocent person, maybe a loving parent who just happened to be in the wrong place at the wrong moment, while the dreadful perpetrator would know he'd gotten away once again, and would rejoice at yet more death and horror caused by his presence in this universe, where his type should not exist in the first place, but they do, and they are part of the Jurassic Yard reality of our existence.

At that horrible, terrifying moment, I started to feel a sense of relief. I had an idea who had done this to me, and I understood the (utterly senseless reasons why). I would never see them again, and thus would be spared any further shattering emotional conflict and yes, they'd get away but that also brought me a sense of liberation, of freedom, because I would get better in a few hours and be more careful next time I went to a bar to have drinks among strangers. A lesson learned. And I could tell my story to hotel security so that maybe they also would be wiser next time.

I remembered the cell phone, and looked down.

Not that I could have summoned the concentration or coordination to call my friends.

The cell phone, in any case, had fallen into a puddle of water near the garden hose at the edge of the patio, and was dead and drowned. A bubble sat trapped in its plastic face, and I could be sure its interior was entirely underwater and short-circuited. In fact, I could hear sputtering, sparking noises. So much for calling. I was on my own for however long it took for this hallucinogenic event to pass.

I was not done yet with this madness.

4. She

Everything I'd ever read, studied, or heard suddenly flashed through my mind in that moment.

It was so painfully clear to me now that your peaceful yard is actually a dinosaur world in which every living thing must survive, must protect itself and its young, while hunting to kill other species. That includes humans, who possess the enzymes to be omnivorous (everything-eaters) as both carnivores (meat eaters) and herbivores (plant eaters).

We humans blossomed, like both flowers covering a meadow, and pond scum thickly choking water. For eons, our numbers remained low, in the few thousands, desperately running from every predator around every corner (including each other). In the Holocene Epoch (the past ten thousand years or so, after the end of the so-called Stone Ages and the last glaciations to date) our numbers rose by a few hundred million in Roman times to about one billion around 1800 and two billion a little after 1925 and three billion (ballooning ever more rapidly, every few years now) after 1950, and then another billion every decade or so, to approach eight billion by 2019 (Blade Runner Year). Not to mention, as we health workers and science types tend to be aware, a million aircraft in the air every minute, and a billion vehicles on the world's roads every hour of every day, are creating a Greenhouse Effect that is sending global temperatures ever more rapidly upward. Since more than half of us live in towns and cities on the shores of lakes, rivers, and oceans, that means flooding and storm surges... and those who try to run will be overwhelmed by disease, starvation, and violence.

Climate change has been around since the beginning of our world (billions of years). Climate factors (warming, cooling, etc) move in changes that are sometimes predictable and sometimes not. The rise of human overpopulation, and the destruction of most large species in what is called the Sixth (and Final?) Great Extinction, combine with carbon emissions and other overwhelming factors to bring us to the end of our world.

There was a great natural warming, for example, from roughly about 850 to around 1350 CE (or A.D.) depending on where you looked, that warmed the European Medieval period, allowing England to be a net wine exporter.

This was followed by a natural great cooling (the Little Ice Age) from (again rough numbers) about 1350 to about 1850, when the Thames in London regularly froze over, and in Charles Dickens' time people could often ice skate on the Thames and have sit-down picnics in the middle of the river.

Around 1750, the human population began reaching new heights, even as our growing science and technology started to kick off the Industrial Revolution. So, even as a few more cold snaps kicked in (the last around 1850) by 1800 or so, the newly bloated cities surrounded by choking smoke and smog started to help a new global warming period kick in. There are lots of factors that I couldn't even think of in my hallucinogenic state as I stood silently screaming for those few minutes on the patio, but I also knew this. If humans had not been blowing smoke, cutting down vast forests, and poisoning rivers and oceans, the new warming period would have naturally passed. But the wealthy oligarchs making huge fortunes vested in coal, oil, and the like are not interested in saving the world. They know they will die, like everyone does, and they are not thinking of future generations, but only about having as much wealth in their pathetic little lives, now and in the short term, and to hell with everything and everyone who comes after them. As King Louis XIV of France said of his lavish lifestyle leading to disaster under his successors (Number 15 and 16, who was beheaded along with his wife Marie Antoinette): "After me, the deluge." He might just as well have said: "After I'm gone, what do I care? Bring on the end of the world for all that I care."

All of those ideas and figures flashed through my head,

even as I prayed to return to my normal state of being. I longed to escape from this nightmare of lucid vision that was in the same moment so dark and foreboding, so Gothic and merciless. I longed to spend the last hours or days or years of our time on this dying planet in blissful oblivion. Maybe if we all flew in dirigibles and used gravitational force to move us most of the way rather than burning fossil fuels (deadly coal, deadly oil), and if we stopped using all that plastic, we could slow down the pace of global destruction. It's probably too late already, unless every living man, woman, and child does their utmost to pitch in (and votes the polluters, the liars, and killers out of office, and stops the oligarchs who pay zillions of bribes and corruption to the liars in positions of influence.

All of that flashed through my head in seconds.

That's what the drug does to you: hallucinogenic dramas and movies of whatever is in your mind already, and in my case it's a mosaic of Emergency Room experiences plus History reading plus what really goes on in that sunny, peaceful yard outside where the bees drone and the flowers smell so sweet.

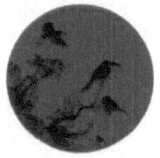

I screamed and started to run from my beautiful patio in a panic.

Why? I didn't even stop to look. Panic and terrified running are the natural order of things for all species, except for us complacent humans who have done away with all of our predators—except those of our fellow humans who have no soul and prey on us with the heartless pleasure of spiders waiting in their webs and grinning in anticipation of the next victim, the next meal, the next bit of fun.

I ran, and had next to no idea where I was going.

As long as I was on the run, I was (almost) safe.

Yes, I could run into a trap, or another predator might be faster and catch up with me...

Running in terror felt great all of a sudden.

Instinct kicked in, and I realized that I would only stop running when I had found the other great thing: a place to hide.

Every bird, every animal, every insect knows these things totally. Not through reasoning, but through instinct, which is basically reasoning cold-wired into their DNA and thus into their brains by evolution. And yes, gravitation, evolution, and climate change are fundamental laws of nature that stand the test of reason and cannot be denied by irrational, ignorant, illogical wishful thinking.

That's why I call myself a trans-Christian. I believe in the Gospel of Love taught by the real Christ in Judaea thousands of years ago, which shines through the Scriptures no matter how they have been twisted and warped by human power structures political, religious, or cultural. That message tells me all people everywhere are the same (good ones, bad ones, mostly nice and helpful ones, with those few rotten apples like my drink poisoner tossed into the mix). I'm comfortable in any house of worship or no house for that matter, unless they start talking hate and nonsense, usually to make the rich richer and the poor dumber and poorer. Nobody has the world's only true religion or they only real magic. Nobody has the only correct translation of ancient wisdoms. Nobody has the right to murder or hate other people because they have slightly different hocus-pocus. No matter how hard you believe in your shtick, until your little brain begins to hum and warm up and smell like burning rubber, nothing changes reality even the tiniest little bit. It's all for nothing. Or better yet, it's all for the benefit of the manipulators who prey on simple people who live in that village in sight of the scary city of Babylon, like in Gen. 2, where those 'others' (shudder!) speak 'different languages' ('diversity', shudder!) and our stern-faced, harshly reassuring demon promises to build walls to keep them out; or better yet kill them all, using us as the lynch mob, lunch mob, whatever...

...booh-hwah-hah-hah-hah!...

My mad running took me down to the lake, where I didn't stop or speak with anyone.

I probably looked like a woman jogging, still dressed in the shorts and T-shirt that my friends had put on me after I was so sick last night.

I had no money with me, nor my wallet and I.D. cards. I stopped at a public fountain for a long drink of water, since I felt very dry.

My vision was still dark and not cloudy so much as underwater and brownish, like looking through that tea I had been drinking earlier.

I was hungry... and there, on a thick brownstone wall by the lakeside, someone had left a fresh, half-eaten sandwich. I think it was egg salad on toast, with a crush of tomatoes, lettuce, mayo, and a bit of bacon. I scooped it up with one hand without slowing down. I didn't hear anyone yelling for my blood or anything. See, we're all predators. We just buy our lunch if we can, rather than kill the prey... well, you get the picture.

I ran some distance and then hid (that old evolutionary instinct) at the end of another brownstone wall, and devoured my kill. Like that hawk with the dead bird in its claws, the trick is to eat fast and then run some more. The hawk had his wings to protect himself; I needed the wall to hide behind.

I began running again, without any idea of where to.

Just to run, to survive, to live another moment...

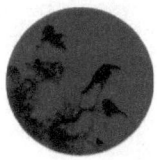

As the doctor had told Dori, and she relayed it to me, this new drug is a powerful hallucinogen. That means it gives birth (*genesis,* from Greek, origin) to strong hallucinations (from a Latin word for dreaming). Hallucinations come from both outside (things we see along the way) and inside (memories of things we have seen or learned).

This trip was taking me through a vivid library of everything I'd ever learned. It explained a lot.

As I continued my breathless jogging, past the lake and into a deep forest, I was reminded of that old Bambi story. The whole flick rattled (like an old-fashioned movie reel) and chattered and flashed through my mind in a few blurry moments as I continued running from the lake and into the forest.

I was amazed at my own strength and endurance, until I realized that I had become transformed.

I saw my reflection clearly in a forest pond, and was both exhilarated and terrified.

I was exhilarated because I saw there a new me: a powerful, giant creature that hardly any other animal or predator (including our species) would want to attack.

In the same moment, I was terrified because the creature I saw, which was myself, had become something part bird and part reptile, almost resembling imagined reconstructions of raptor dinosaurs like T. Rex, Allosaurus, and their kind. Whatever I had become, I was a species *a sui generis*, in my own kind, crafted by the hallucinogens from fragments of knowledge surviving in my memory.

I had large hind limbs on which I could run forever. My forelimbs were small and relatively weak, with claws designed for minor work. The major work (of attacking, tearing, and devouring) was to be done by my enormous, almost car-sized head full of enormous, razor-sharp teeth. My oddly bird-like overall form was covered in a fine layer of down and the ancestors of evolving feathers. You laugh. I laugh at the memory. I was a killer chicken the size of a small dump truck.

The Woman rides, and How!

5. Babylon

I came onto a road, which was offset by houses and driveways on either side.

Gradually, that road led to a wider one, almost a highway, which led into a city of tall buildings, with great bridges over a river, and soaring domes and spires.

Amid the darkness and the fog, what I most heard was a constant mournful howling like that of air raid sirens warning of an impending bomb attack or other catastrophe.

You ask: so did people see you and laugh in the city?

No, to my surprise, half-crazed as I was, because they streets were empty. The city itself, whose buildings were dotted with thousands of points of light, was shrouded in a mist like a marine layer at the sea. A brooding, oppressive, damp shroud of fog lay over the streets and strangled the bottom stories of skyscrapers. I ran, unchallenged and unopposed, down the middle of deserted streets. There were a few cars, mostly parked at the curbs as if suddenly abandoned by terrified drivers. In a few places I hopped over a car or motorcycle left in the middle of the street.

Always there was that constant howling all around of rising and falling sirens...

As I ran, I realized that this entire city and its culture were manifestations of our human territorial tyranny. Everything had to do with territory, ;possession, property. It was all: *this is mine and you can't have it, or else*. It's all about who owns what. Those who own a lot allow those who don't to work for them, without ever owning the store or business where the work is done. Payment (sharing) is in artificial, symbolic food scraps known as money.

This whole place, Babylon, was really the imprinted yard, inversion of the Eden myth, implanted in the human mind, a memory maybe of some dinosaurian swamp a quarter billion years ago. Mammals did not exist yet, but DNA and RNA did, in tiny wriggling virus or bacteria life forms that would eventually grow bigger and more complex and successful, some of them to be modeled on the early-birds swooshing around those deadly swamps looking for lunch…

I stood in the middle of the city, in a green plaza, and raised my head up to roar with open mouth into the sky.

It was my turn to roar.

My voice echoed for miles. I could hear it bouncing back on itself as it reached my ears on the return. Power is everything.

I joined the sirens howling, and my voice rose above theirs.

I was The Woman, and I was hunting.

Grab your ass with both hands and run for your life, because I am coming down the street looking for you, Mr. Swastika.

I had gone from being a terrified woman standing in a suddenly transformed garden at the time share by the lake—to being the most powerful predator in this city of ancient name.

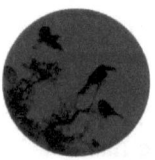

Catching a scent in the air, I sniffled curiously.

I stopped howling long enough to assess the situation.

I bowed my massive head and sniffed more energetically.

Deep inside, I felt a thrill of rage and revenge.

I began trotting, then running, along the streets of the city toward a river.

At first, the river was a black ribbon shining with moonlight.

As I drew near, I saw that there were a few men standing around a car.

They had a stereo playing from multiple speakers, and hopped about dancing and laughing.

As I drew near, I began to sniff their scent, and it seemed familiar.

I was so fast they did not see me coming.

I ran silently and purposefully, like an express train on its gleaming tracks.

The men were dancing about, triumphantly, and laughing.

Their sound was cold, cruel, and merciless.

One of them had a partially shaved head with a swastika. The other three had tattoos on their necks, which I recognized from my fleeting, deeply buried memories of that wonderful bar, which they ruined by poisoning me with date rape drugs.

They saw me coming, and froze in terror. Their leader, like the rest of them, instantly lost all of his arrogance and became a simpering, helpless coward. In seconds, I snapped my powerful jaws around them. I tossed my head and threw bits and bloody pieces of them in all directions. As I shredded and pulped them, I roared so that the city echoed with my rage and triumph. Finally breathless, and there was so little of them to begin with, I ambled down to the river and thrust my head into its cool waters to clean myself of their filth. I left their car sitting where it was, but only after I stomped on it a few times to silence that obnoxious music. From there, I felt deflated, as if all purpose had gone out of me.

Certainly, my rage was spent. I was tired...

So I started walking back the way I had come through that ever darker, deep-brown mist...

John T. Cullen

6. Eden

...I awakened, lying on my side on the patio back at the time share condo, as if nothing (much) had happened. Well, except for the cell phone that lay dying and sputtering in muddy water, and a bunch of torn leaves and twigs were scattered all around as if I'd been in a mighty struggle during my sleep. I lay in a heap, and the patio around me was a debris field. Not a bird twittered nor a bee droned. I must have terrified them all with my hollering and thrashing.

Voices prodded me from my deeply unconscious sleep.

"Alina!"

"Girl, what are you doing!"

"For god's sake, are you okay?"

Dori and Sheri and Laura came running. I could hear their sweet heels on the slate patio.

Sheri and Laura lifted me into a sitting position, while Dori felt my pulse at one wrist.

"Should we call an ambulance?" Laura asked.

Dori frowned. "Get her into the deck chair over there. Her pulse is strong, and I'm not sure it's anything more than another hallucination like the MD said."

The girls, my dear friends, helped me upright.

I was shaky, but I waved them off. "I'll be okay."

They insisted on helping me walk to the deck chair, where I had originally sat.

Wow, what an ordeal.

"We tried calling," Sheri said, "but your phone seemed to be dead."

"It's lying in a puddle, shorted to death," Dori said.

"I'm sorry," I said. "I must have dropped it."

"You were dreaming, girl," Sheri said.

"Well guess what," Dori said. "Over in the city, there's a big police action going on. They have found four men who were seen at the bar last night. Someone or something tore them to bloody shreds. There is nothing left but messy pulp, along with shoes, underpants, and some tattooed skin. Whatever it was, it must have been huge and almost ate them while it tore them to pieces."

Laura added: "Police said on the news that the men had a bottle of date rape pills in their glove compartment."

Dori said: "As a nurse, I called up the police and explained our situation. I told them to check and see if for sure it was the same thing they slipped in your drink."

I cleared my throat as Sheri handed me a glass of water to drink. "I'm sure it was," I said quietly.

The three women looked at me a bit puzzled, amid all that crazy news.

"How can you be so calm and so sure?" Dori asked while kneeling near the foot of the deck chair.

I shrugged, and looked around me at the world.

The fog had cleared.

Sunshine, balmy air, rustling palm trees, it was all back to normal.

Sailboats prettied up the blue lake water, which twinkled with many borrowed patches of light, much as the city in my hallucination had shone with thousands of yellowish windows in the fog.

Bees droned about. Little birds darted here and there. Lizards wriggled on a warm garden wall.

"It's good to be alive," I said quietly. "We have a lot of work to do to make sure and keep this world going the way we know and love it."

My three friends rose up, and Dori declared: "Yeah, she's feeling better."

"You're going to be fine," Sheri assured me, and Laura nodded.

Dory's cell phone warbled, and she sat at the table to take the call. We all looked at her as she nodded, with a serious face, and eyes that brightened as truth became clearer. "Thank you," she said and rang off. Then she told us: "That was the head of security at the hotel. They looked through the surveillance cams from the halls and at the bar that night. The dead guys by the river are the same ones who showed up at the bar and stood right near you, Alina. The drugs in their car were the same new type, very rare, that they dropped in your champagne."

"Case solved," Laura said.

"Oh man," Sheri said, "I'll never go anywhere alone again."

I added: "Yeah, and hold your drink close, and keep a hand over it to protect yourself."

We all took a deep breath, and let out one huge collective sigh.

"We have a few days left here before we go home," Dori said.

"We can still enjoy ourselves," Sheri said.

"Eyes wide open," Laura said.

I said to all of them, and nobody in particular: "Older and wiser in a hurry, for sure. Isn't this yard just glorious?"

Butterflies danced and flapped in their colorful dance. A cute little hummingbird poked its beak in a red blossom while hunting around for a safe spot to build a nest. Two big blackbirds had a learned discussion up in a tree crown. A prowling fluffy, black and white cat stopped to look up at them with green eyes, decided not to argue with their moral position, and instead blinked patiently, and then went to find his favorite toy to play with. And that's what we all did that day. We put the insane movie (Bambi meets Adolf) behind us, and prettied up to go out and enjoy the rest of our time by those blue sparkling waters with their red and blue and white sails, and the aromas of fresh baked lunch drifting through the balmy air while palm trees rustled and the occasional passenger jet left a silent contrail high up in a perfectly blue sky.

Epilog

As told by Alina, we saw the true-life, historical relationship of monstrous Adolf Hitler with *Bambi, A Life in the Woods*. That classic story by Felix Salten was forbidden by Hitler's terrifying Jurassic regime that led to about 100 million human deaths and a generation devastated around the world.

Like Alina's story, Bambi has its dark side—sanitized by cartoon makers, but we dig deeper and the reality is right there in the original story.

Let's discuss the title, *Jurassic Backyard*, which I playfully adapted from a famous novel, movie, and franchise by one of our creative heroes: Michael Crichton.

We honor the genius of Michael Crichton, whose superb entertainments (often with philosophical underpinnings) include the epic *Jurassic Park*. My favorite Crichton novel, actually, was *Congo*. The great man said once in an interview that he didn't like to write characters so much...whatever he meant by that, because story cannot succeed without characters, and he wrote those quite well for story purposes. The two children in *Jurassic Park* may well be the best delineated in that novel. But my vote for all-time best Chrichton character goes to Amy, the gorilla in *Congo*.

As it happens, I used to subscribe long ago to the now-extinct SFFH magazine *Omni*, whose every issue had a small section of silvery pages up front, dedicated (as I recall now, many years later) to a collection of the latest little news blips from science, technology, the arts, and so forth. One of those little articles, in a 1980s issue, was a short piece to the effect that one day, it might be possible to clone dinosaurs from DNA captured in primordial amber.

Over a hundred million years ago, when the great (avians, more than lizards) prowled the earth, roaring and chewing on screaming smaller creatures, there were flies buzzing happily about. These flies, like their contemporaries today, found great solace and nurture in poop. They ate it, they danced on it, they held meetings on it... Such offal would include dinosaur doodles. A fly that had recently dined on dino doo might well find itself trapped a while later in a rivulet of golden sap running down the side of a tree. That sap is the stuff from which nature millions of years ago created precious amber. If you find a Jurassic fly trapped in amber, you might theoretically be able to extract not only its insect DNA, but also the DNA of whatever it ate last, which might include a drop of dinosaur blood or whatever...

I remember thinking, as I read the article, what a great idea for a story. Even though I'd been writing speculative fiction for years, more in a poetic and surrealistic vein (adorations of Edgar Allan Poe, Ray Bradbury, Cordwainer Smith, and Jorge Luis Borges to name just a handful), I could not think of how to make a story from that notion.

Michael Crichton, a brilliant and versatile thinker, did so on his soaring wings of imagination. In an interview many years later, he told of being inspired by that very same little item in *Omni* to write what became the great *Jurassic Park* franchise. I saved the magazine for my idea collection, but that was as far as I got with the notion. Bully for Michael. I'm sorry we lost him at a relatively young age, for he would have given us many other delights. He died at age 66 in 2008 of lymphoma, a blood cancer. I will mention (think of *Congo*; think of *The Thirteenth Warrior*, a 1999 movie based on his historical epic *Eaters of the Dead*) that Michael Crichton was probably the only successful mainstream author who wrote novels that were weighted with footnotes and endnotes. He was an intellectual, after all. And it worked, I might add. Only Michael could pull something like that off.

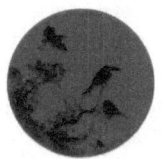

Actually, the germ of this story (*Jurassic Backyard*) came to me uniquely, years ago in a different context. I was sitting in our idyllic little yard in sunny, balmy San Diego. No matter where on earth we live (and I've lived many places in my lifetime, both in North America and in several European countries), we are all familiar with the joy of a sunny backyard filled with blooming, fragrant flowers, twittering birds, chirping insects, and dashing little lizards. We enjoy the colorful dance of butterflies, the antics of a prowling cat, and the nuzzling of a busy, productive little bee. It all seems so peaceful and idyllic, doesn't it?

One day, it occurred to me that these tranquil scenes are simply the product of our apex predator status on a planet, in a universe, built upon the joys, the terrors, and the beauty of life's two primary vectors: survival, and procreation.

In fact, the prowling cat is on the lookout to make a kill (and avoid being eaten by a sneaky coyote). The birds, twittering, are actually signaling to each other in terror, male and female; gang members, if you've heard those raucous crows, ravens, and bluejays. In our backyard, not far from the San Diego River and about eight miles from the Pacific Ocean, we daily witness turf battles as flocks of big, raucous crows gang up to drive away soaring hawks looking for their own hunting opportunities.

Watch a male-female pair of smaller birds nesting, and you'll see the most amazing survival techniques. One will sit in the well-hidden nest over their brood, while the other goes looking for food; and when that mate brings back lunch, he or she does not fly directly to the nest, which would be giving the whole show away to a predatory hawk or crow (or whatever); rather, the food bringer will alight on a rooftop chimney ten or more meters away, look about nervously to make sure he or she isn't being observed, and only then make a zig-zag dash for the nest where hubby is waiting. All of nature is full of this survival maneuvering, like a great roller skating rink throbbing with danger and terror.

We are now at our most perilous way station in the early 21st Century. We dominate the world, yet we live in daily fear. Our main source of terror comes not from cats or coyotes, but from our fellow humans. That's why we lock our windows and doors at night or when away; why some may think about owning a gun or a baseball bat; and why we avoid going to parts of town with a certain reputation; why we don't leave the house much after dark.

When I was in Basic Training (U.S. Army, Fort Ord, CA) last century, we were under instructions to never, after hours or on weekend pass, ever walk anywhere alone on post. We were subject to arrest by the Military Police if a squad car happened to see an individual walking alone on a street. Penalties included confinement to barracks, and financial fines (Article 15). Too many bad things happen to the individual, even on a major military post. So that's life, not only in the big city, but out over the treeline on the horizon. Welcome to everyone's own Jurassic Backyard.

We have in our own DNA a pastiche of many species when it comes to this, including primates, birds, lizards, and insects. Long story, for another day and another writing, but next time you sit in your easy chair on the patio, overlooking your yard or canyon or trees while reading a book or playing with your phone, listen to the sounds of desperation, struggle, and in the end death or survival amid the twittering and butterfly beauty.

The definitive notion came to me one day, on my daily pilgrimage to Barnes & Noble for coffee and books. Among my degrees is a B.A. in Literature, so I cannot help myself but to spend a lifetime studying what makes stories and poetry tick. It dawned on me, as I stood looking at a field of the best gathered *florilegia*, flowers of writing, that it all boils down to this. We are born, we strive, and yes we pass ultimately into the same unknown that claims birds, cats, primates, comets, and galaxies. We are stardust, we are golden, as the popular tune of my youth in the 1960s gladly intoned. But it boils down to one thing: mating, so that we can reproduce our DNA and leave a legacy (hard-wired into us). To that end, we must fight for survival, which includes gathering some protective territory in which two of us—a man and a woman—can mate and produce offspring, which in the best case scenario, ideally, we then nurture and raise to become the next generation while our train moves on into that same tunnel seen at the conclusion of at least one famous Alfred Hitchcock movie. It's all metaphor, right? But reality also.

The point of all this was driven home when I played the radio in my car while driving home. Sure enough, there it was on every station: loud rock music in all of its genres, about 99% of it dedicated to mating. "I'm looking for you everywhere..." and "You left me broken-hearted..." and so on. You know the instinctive themes as well as I do. We all do.

In my story Jurassic Backyard, I offer a dramatization of my vision, namely that our yard—your backyard, with its colorful butterflies and singing birds and other charming fellow travelers in this life—is really a war zone. It is a jungle, like in Jurassic times.

This is food for thought for thoughtful readers, while it is predictably terrifying to readers prefer cartoon visions of life. I understand it all. I was a child once. I sat in a movie theater in Europe as a child, and cried while Bambi sobbed with his head nestled against his dying mother's side, and The Man (a dark, cruel, heartless hunter killing animals for his own sheer Jurassic enjoyment) laughed in the distance, like a tyrannosaur roaring triumphantly at the clouds above.

Not long ago, right here in my peaceful neighborhood in San Diego (Grantville), I was working late when, about 1:50 a.m., I heard a series of popping sounds. Being a U.S.

Army veteran, I know the sound of gunfire. The sequence went "pop-pop-pop-pop-pop-PAUSE-pop." Being a long-ago newspaper reporter, I automatically noted the time of the event. I listened a while longer, expecting to hear police sirens. *Nothing…*

Was I wrong? Was it just someone playing with firecrackers? The night slumbered on peacefully, and I went to bed.

Next morning, I woke to learn that a young man had been shot to death a few streets away near the neighborhood park. To date (2020, Vision Year) his killer has not yet been identified.

I called police and spoke with them about my observation (actually: hearing), and they thanked me for that minor contribution, which helped their investigation. My description, which they agreed with, sticks in my memory: "There were a series of slowly, deliberate, evenly spaced popping sounds, followed by a PAUSE, and one last POP." That would have been the murderer stepping in close to give his victim one last bullet—the execution shot. The young man died there in the street after that final POP. We don't yet know why he had come to this normally quiet neighborhood, presumably to meet his killer for some reason. We can guess all day (drug deal?). We may never know, although sometimes the truth surfaces years later through some trivial connected fact, usually someone who knew something but was afraid to tell. And that is just one Jurassic moment in this peaceful-seeming modern age.

Think of Alina's story, like Lord of the Flies; or for that matter, Robinson Crusoe—the real story, as written by Daniel Defoe 1719, a dark tale of cannibalism, murder, betrayal, and terror unlike the fuzzy-bunny Disney cartoons dolled down to narcotic innocence.

So here is a story about one such yard, and one young woman, engaged as we all are in the daily joys and struggles of which I have spoken; of which all literature, all music, all the arts, and even scriptures speak to us, or we speak through them.

Aristotle, in his *Poetics*, suggested that there is a twofold purpose to every work of art. That is, to entertain, and to edify (teach). As any modern artist knows, the entertainment is primary, and the edification is a welcome hitch-hiker on the back of pleasure.

To that I would add: the finest entertainment actually delivers on three levels, the ultimate of which lies in the atmospherics, the richness, the poetic strength by which it rises above craftmanship (itself a noble form at its best) to the stratosphere of true artistry. For example, my favorite movie is the 1982 Ridley Scott SF classic Blade Runner, which I like to invoke in describing the meaning of my own subgenre definition DarkSF. More on that in a moment.

Image: Argo Navis, Johannes Hevelius 1690, courtesy Wikimedia (Maxim Razin)

This story, like most of my speculative fiction (SF),

was originally published under the pseudonym John Argo.

I chose that pen name in 1996 when I first started publishing works online. The Argo reference was for the ship of wonder, Argo, on which the heroes of the Bronze Age sailed forth into the outer space of their day—namely, the Aegean and Pontic Seas, and ultimately the Mediterranean Sea and even the near Atlantic Ocean.

Added (relevant) Note: Speaking of Jurassic predators, as I write this, I am simultaneously enduring a lengthy wait time on the phone. I'm working with my credit union to repair the damage done by an unknown hacker who stole my credit information (presumably at a gas station), and hacked my account for over $500 at some remote store. It is taking me hours of phone time, frustration, on line struggles, and at least one visit to the credit union to undo what a kind lady at the Social Security Administration called "cruelty."

How true her words are. The silent predators who stalk us have no regard for their fellow human beings. It's another example of the Jurassic Backyard that borders our desired world of safety, sanity, and kindness. Luckily most people fall into the latter category. It's the small number of ferocious yet icy human sociopaths who spoil it for us all.

Oddly enough, we seem to enjoy reading novels and watching movies about these creatures. See for example my short novel *Terror In My Arms,* in which we encounter yet another guy and his female victim. Available at Amazon in print and ebook as *Terror In My Arms* by John T. Cullen.

About Author & Works

For readers who are interested, I will close with some highlights of my writing history, in hope that readers will be inspired to look more deeply into my works. I won't offer the standard list of (my fifty) books, as found in most books. All that is available (with sample reading) at my webplex.

My web presence (since 1996) includes my personal site at www.johntcullen.com plus my publisher website at www.clocktowerbooks.com.

I was editor and publisher for ten years of a pioneering SFFH professional magazine, originally titled *Deep Outside SFFH*, and later renamed *Far Sector SFFH*. We published work by authors including SFWA officers, and also men and women who earned (or were nominated for) every major prize in the SF world, including Hugos, Nebulas, and Sturgeons; plus famous U.K. and Commonwealth prizes. The magazine in its two iterations ran from 1998 to 2007.

When I first realized the potential in digital and online publishing, I was overcome by a sense of wonder. In fact, 'Sense of Wonder' is a classic way that SF enthusiasts (writers, publishers, editors, critics) have described the highest emotional payoff in this type of literature.

Like all labels, 'imaginative literature' is a bit of a misnomer, since by its nature all literature is imaginative. We're typically talking about publishing categories and pigeon-holes.

When I was about to start publishing my novels online in early 1996, I thought about what name I should use.

Should I use my European birth name Jean-Thomas Cullen? Or the U.S. handle I use in the English speaking world, John T. Cullen?

Quick light shed on that: when I was a senior in high school, an elderly aunt living in Meriden, CT urged me to apply to nearby Wesleyan University, along with my two or three other applications. I was a bit out to lunch, in a world of my own, and not thinking much about the future. My grades and tests were solid, I was a published poet at 18, a working newspaper reporter (summer interne) at 17, and a first-novelist at 19, so I did have a few things going for me. I applied to Wesleyan (not picking on them; could happen anywhere) and visited their campus one day. All very nice, until a letter arrived: "Dear Jean, we are very impressed with your achievements and we would love to have you here as a student, but Wesleyan does not accept girls." It was 1968.

Really. My aunt got on that immediately (ten minute drive from Meriden to Middletown, where there also is famously the main nut house in CT). I got a letter of apology from Wesleyan, stating they had placed my name on their waiting list for acceptance, should one of the admitted students drop out.. It is a very desirably university, and no openings actually appeared. So I attended the University of Connecticut at its sprawling Storrs campus.

Back to the name game: in 1996 I was overcome with a sense of wonder about the limitless potential of what we then called the World Wide Web (WWW), today more commonly the Internet.

From my Classics background, I summoned wonderful memories of mythology, to wit: Jason and the Argonauts. Jason and his crew on the ship Argo (literally, they were Argo-Sailors, or Argo-Nauts). They sailed the galaxy of their day, long ago during the misty, distant Bronze Age, as told and retold in Classical Hellas (Greece) a thousand years later, and ever after. In fact, people are today still making movies about Jason and the Argo Sailors, including their adventures in finding the Golden Fleece while fighting hordes of zombies, ghosts, cannibals, and aliens. In our day and age, we think about adventures in outer space. In their time (ancient by the time of Homer, Hesiod, and Herodotus already) outer space more likely meant the remote waters of the Aegean, or of the Pontic (Black) Sea, or the western Mediterranean or even the nearby Atlantic regions.

That is why I chose John Argo as my pseudonym for category fiction.

Argo (or *Argo Navis*, Argo Ship) was for centuries also the name of the largest constellation in the Southern Skies, as seen from Europe. In recent centuries, astronomers have broken the ship up into its major component parts, so that we have Puppis (stern or poop deck; see the etymological connection); Vela (sail); and Carina (keel).

I thought I was on to something, back then in the late 1990s, before the arrival of e-commerce, identity theft, and every imaginable other type of cyber-crime. It really was, for a brief time, an age of wonder, a kind of Argo-age, when a small crew of us sailed the Bronze Age Web in search of adventure.

I had a small but avid global readership in the late 1990s. Then, in the early 2000s at Fictionwise, I and my then-Clocktower Books authors had a second breath of wind. For a year or two, I practically owned the Nonfiction/History section, sometimes claiming all top ten slots for most popular nonfiction. For a while, also, I did really well in the fiction slots, but that began predictably to fade when I became just one of a million struggling authors. But I had my heyday, and I still know how to crank 'em out. If anyone is interested. *Nudge, nudge…*

Working passionately online for about a quarter century now (1996), I have built a network (like a model train set) of numerous interlinked websites, including at least one each for my poetry, my fiction, and my nonfiction. There is also a Clocktower Books Museum site, plus an online shopping center (*Citta Moda*) that I built as an

Amazon affiliate since about 2000.

I would recommend that readers begin by visiting Galley City (www.galleycity.com), where one can read most of my novels half for free on a try-buy basis. More on that below. Look for the Bookstore Metaphor and Read-a-Latte.

I published the world's first true e-book online (suspense thriller *Neon Blue, or Girl, Unlocked*) and the SF novel *This Shoal of Space* (also 1996). Criteria for that claim: (1) proprietary, not public domain, thus ruling out Gutenberg and the like; (2) entire, not samples; (3) entirely online in HTML format, not on portable media like floppies or CD, which a few souls did about the same time; (4) innovative format of weekly chapters published sequentially, always on a Sunday afternoon PST for readers around the world to enjoy as they came to work and enjoyed their morning coffee or tea; (5) available TXT downloads of the whole novel if, as often happened, readers in South Africa or West Germany or New Zealand or Taiwan or Canada or USA or (a lot of points around the world) could not stand the suspense and needed to know immediately how the story ended.

I like to tell what I call the 'Copyshop Story,' something that happened to me more than once, and has been quite gratifying.

One day, long ago, an agent requested to see my suspense novel *Neon Blue* (or: *Girl, Unlocked*).

In those days, you were expected to make a copy on a copier (as in a copy shop); we didn't quite have today's widespread use of PDF copies and so forth.

I went to a large copyshop in my neighborhood, which offered one-hour service. I walked in with my 400 page typewritten manuscript, and found the store jammed with customers (a Friday afternoon, as I recall). Not only that but there was only one person behind the counter, the owner of the franchise store, who was trying to serve a dozen customers while doing innumerable tasks at the same time.

When I finally reached the counter and explained that I needed one copy of my novel, she gave me a frazzled look. "My big copier is broken," she said, "so I can't run your copy automatically. If you can wait, I'll have it for you tomorrow. I'll make your copy one sheet at a time on the small copier."

I thanked her, said that would be fine, and left the ms for her to work on that evening.

The next morning, a Saturday, I walked in to pay and collect my work. The place was empty, and there on the counter sat two manuscripts side by side: my original and one copy.

"Good morning," I said.

"I hate you," she said, while doing work toward the rear of the store. She gave me a sidelong glance.

I felt rather shocked. "Huh?"

"Yes," she said. "I was making your copy one sheet at a time on the small copying machine. I started reading, and could not stop. So I ended up taking your novel home, and reading all night. I hardly slept at all, and I'm dead tired today. So I hate you." Then she added, with a happy glow: "Do you have another one like it, that I can read?"

I got it now, that wry sense of humor. We had a good laugh together. I was pleased (this has happened to me more than once) that she liked the novel well enough to ask for another such story from me. That's the highest form of praise, I think. In a world of struggle and discouragement, as most authors experience too often, that is a really nice thing to hear. And it's a story I still love to tell, all these years later. Because, again, it has happened to me more times than I can count, in different settings.

Now I'll discuss the short novel at hand, *Jurassic*

Backyard, written in 2019; or novela, novella, novelette, whatever; I call it *venti*, Italian for twenty, meaning a twenty-something word count range.

Jurassic Backyard is a short work of DarkSF Fantasy.

The original 2019 title was *Jurassic Yard*, which is a sort of consonant eye-rhyme with *Jurassic Park*. The new title (*Jurassic Backyard*) better describes the metaphor: your backyard as a combat zone in a constant life and death struggle among insects, lizards, plants (competing for soil and sunlight), birds, and mammals.

The neighborhood kids used to watch the 1989 comedy hit *Honey I Shrunk the Kids* over and over again. By extension, I saw the movie (and had a lot of fun) several times. Seemed a bit of a take on *The Incredible Shrinking Man*, 1957 movie based on a Richard Matheson SF novel.

Nothing wrong with that. Artists do borrow from each other. Ovid, great Roman poet in the age of Augustus, compiled and reworked many classic poems, among them a then already ancient Babylonian story called *Pyramus and Thisbe* (a love story, tragic ending) that ultimately, about two thousand years after its (probable, if not earlier) creation morphed into Shakespeare's *Romeo and Juliet* (which brilliant Willie cribbed from several contemporary French and Italian novels of same theme). That's just one example of many.

So: What is DarkSF? Why do I use that term?

I like to say that "DarkSF is the dark chocolate of speculative fiction."

By SF, furthermore, I mean SFFH—the combined categories called rather arbitrarily science fiction, fantasy, and horror (however publishers and retailers may arrange them for commercial purposes).

DarkSF is not intended to be gory, slasher, scary, or in any way juvenile.

Rather, I think of DarkSF in terms of the highest art (poetry, stories, films) that not only entertains us, but that comes wrapped in its own rich cloud of atmosphere and nuance.

DarkSF is the Dark Chocolate of Speculative Fiction.

Some favorite examples from film include, at the top, the 1982 film *Blade Runner*, my all-time favorite movie. Like so much superior fare, it was misunderstood and disliked by many at first, whereas I fell in love with it on first sight, before I was even halfway through watching Ridley Scott's masterpiece for the first time.

This is really the meaning of my three goals in art: to teach, to entertain, and to raise up or transform the audience to a state of awe and bliss. Granted, those things mean different things to different individuals, but we can indeed reach some consensus on the likes of Rainer Maria Rilke, or Paul Verlaine, or Leonardo da Vinci for example.

In that realm, speaking of SF, I think highly of such wonderful fare as *Dark City*, or the French SF film *Chrysalis*. The classic *Metropolis* (Fritz Lang, 1927) was derided in its day, but like *Blade Runner*, is now considered by many connoisseurs to be one of the finest films ever made.

On the fiction side in Speculative Fiction (SFFH), I have already mentioned Borges, Bradbury, Cordwainer Smith, and Poe; I can add a lot of other names that fit well, like Samuel Delaney. And, I would easily demonstrate, there are SF (speculative fiction) elements in the Classics, from the *Epic of Gilgamesh* to the *Iliad*, the *Odyssey*, the *Aeneid*, and more. Half of Shakespeare is SF in the broad sense of speculative fiction. Now all fiction can be argued as being speculative, but let's not approach that for now.

For example, in the overall lore of the Iliad, the idea of a wooden horse is a bit of techno-thriller, which in itself can be categorized as science fiction (or at least, techno-fiction); while the gods and goddesses that abound, moving the narrative along, are pure fantasy. And the scary parts are horror, like the Medusa across the spectrum of Hellenic mythology.

ARGO NAVIS

Now I am not of some delusion that my little story *Jurassic Backyard* is of that exalted class. I only claim a minor niche for it as a story that entertains, makes us think, and conveys a certain richness of atmosphere. For more of my own writing (at last fifty books at this point, including poetry and stories), please visit www.galleycity.com where you can read half of most novels free, try-buy, which I call the Bookstore Metaphor. You can sit all day if you wish, and read free as long as you want. By halfway through a book, you'll have a good idea if you want to know how it ends. You may be hungry by then and want to go home, so you might just want to take the book with you (after paying the clerk, of course). Same here, except you can also order the e-book online for the price of a cup of coffee. Best deal in town. A cup of coffee (latte) is gone in minutes, whereas the book stays with your forever. I coined the motto Read-a-Latte for that, as well.

My novels include psychological thrillers like *Terror in My Arms* and historical thrillers like *Lethal Journey* (based on a true crime in Coronado, near San Diego, in the gaslamp era of 1892). I am an Active Member, International Thriller Writers (ITW) and my small (indie) press imprint Clocktower Books, in San Diego, is a recognized ITW publisher.

On the science fiction side, writing mainly as John Argo, I have about twenty novels in print, including the Empire of Time series and a number of DarkSF stand-alones unified by theme and atmosphere. Again, DarkSF is not necessarily horror, and definitely not slasher or gory or cheap thrills, but the Dark Chocolate of Speculative Fiction (SFFH).

My historical fiction includes what I have begun calling Big Romantic Adventure Novels (BRAN). Among those, *Siberian Girl* owes something to Boris Pasternak and

Herman Wouk, to name just two authors. My Euro-thriller *Valley of Seven Castles, a Luxembourg Thriller* is structurally based on John Buchan's 1915 thriller *The Thirty-Nine Steps*, and has some remarkable affinities with Alfred Hitchcock's work (who was enriched by Buchan's work, as I relate in a *Thrillerology* appendix in that novel); but the pacing and story urgency have much to do with the 2003 film *The Bourne Identity* (Franka Potente, Matt Damon) based on a great Robert Ludlum novel by the same title. My political thriller *CON2: The Generals of October* is what I call a Constitution Thriller, based on what would happen if we ever (god forbid) invoke Article V of the U.S. Constitution and hold a Second Constitutional Convention. The atmospherics in *CON2* owe a lot to such classics as *Three Days of the Condor*, *Parallax View*, and above all, *Seven Days in May*.

That's just a partial list of my novels written over the past half century or more, starting with my first complete novel (SF, titled Summer Planets) completed age 19 while a sophomore at the University of Connecticut. I was a published poet by 18, and a working newspaper reporter at 17 (summer interne reporter at *The New Haven Journal-Courier*).

I'll add one key note here: most, if not all, of my fiction includes a strong love story. That is, I have always tended to have a strong male lead and a strong female lead, who fall in love while having an adventure or solving a crime or traveling across the galaxy. In the end, virtually without exception, they overcome their obstacles and find HEA (Happy Ever After).

The only exception, actually, is Lethal Journey, a 1892 period noir (gaslamp era) thriller closely based on a true crime that occurred at the beautiful Hotel del Coronado resort and hotel near San Diego. The true story, involving a mysterious young woman forever remembered as The Beautiful Stranger, starts with a strong (true life) love story but ends in betrayal and tragedy of epic proportions; no fudging that one, although I have a fantasy in work, in which the Beautiful Stranger survives. The story owes nothing to the 1980 cult movie classic *Somewhere in Time* (Christopher Reeve, Jane Seymour) based on the 1975 novel by Richard Matheson titled *Bid Time Return*. By coincidence, Matheson's novel takes place at the Hotel del Coronado. That is the great hotel, which (again, by coincidence) you may remember seeing in the 1959 comedy movie *Some Like It Hot* (Tony Curtis, Marilyn Monroe, Jack Lemmon). After my retirement, I worked there two years part-time as a shuttle driver, which gave me a unique insight into the atmosphere and quality of both the hotel and of Coronado, which lies on an island across San Diego Bay from the beautiful city I have called home for half of my life now.

Speaking of 'one more note,' I cannot help but mention my youthful novel *On Saint Ronan Street*, written as a homesick young (age 27) enlisted soldier stationed with the U.S. Army in West Germany. That novel, and its later accompanying book of my teen and early 20s poetry (Cymbalist Poems), more than forty years later was cloned (by me) to become an entirely new novel titled *Paris Affaire* (praised by *Kirkus Reviews*). Paris Affaire is the exact same story of a struggling young poet and his lover, a beautiful and neglected young university faculty wife. The first version takes place around Yale University in New Haven, CT while the later version (same story, different names and places) takes place in the Left Bank, *Quartier Latin*, and Sorbonne among its Parisian settings. The cloning was inspired when I saw one of those once in a lifetime, amazing movies (French; *The Umbrellas of Cherbourg*). I realized that my 1976 novel had the same sort of downbeat, Gallic romantic melancholia as the *Umbrellas* film with the divine Catherine Deneuve; but at the last moment, I provided Paris Affaire with a very different, upbeat ending that you'll have to read to understand. Three hints: the bells of Notre Dame de Paris Cathedral; the ultimate, passionate kiss on the parvis before that church on the *Île de Paris*; and my young hero's stolen poetry brought to justice…

But enough for now.

Please do visit www.galleycity.com and enjoy the Bookstore Metaphor (Read-a-Latte).

Read half free on a try-buy basis, just as you can sit all day and read for free at most large bookstores. If you like what you are reading, please do buy the book, typically inexpensively like the price of a cup of coffee.

Hence, the Read-a-Latte metaphor. The coffee is gone in minutes, but the book will be with you forever.

I have had great fun posting my own webplex (over a dozen linked websites, including specific ones for my poetry, my fiction, and my nonfiction; as well as my San Diego small press or indie imprint Clocktower Books; and the Clocktower Books museum site documenting highlights of our online presence as digital/ebook pioneers since early 1996; and lots more fun stuff; e.g., a shopping mall, and of course a bookstore with several entries like All Night Books, Caffeine Books, and more). I liked putting together model train sets as a child; now I build a webplex (very similar).

One of my great missed opportunities in life was not going for a Ph.D. in History (my major academic passion, aside from languages and literature). I earned a B.A. in English (Anguish?) from the University of Connecticut. While serving in the U.S. Army in West Germany, I earned an M.S. in Business Admininstration (Boston University; Overseas Div. Heidelberg). Later, employed at a series of Jurassic war plants in SoCal, I added my 'practical degree,' a B.B.A. in Computer Info Systems and Accounting. Yes, all over the map, but with a plan... to entertain you and, in a greater dimension, to serve up food for thought.

Thank you, and Happy Reading.
JTC
San Diego, CA USA
May 2020 (the Vision Year)